Incorcisms
Strange Short Stories

David Hartley

D1421486

ARACHNE PRESS

First published in UK 2021 by Arachne Press Limited
100 Grierson Road, London SE23 1NX
www.arachnepress.com
© David Hartley 2021
ISBNs
Print 978-1-913665-24-1
ePub 978-1-913665-25-8
Mobi/kindle 978-1-913665-26-5
Audio 978-1-913665-59-3

Thanks to Muireann Grealy for her proofing.
Thanks to Camille Smithwick for her cover design.

Printed on Woodfree paper by TJ Books, Padstow.

The publication of this book is supported using public funding by the National Lottery through Arts Council England

Acknowledgements

Daylight Savings, first published in *Dusk*, Arachne Press 2018
Help Yourself, first published on Reflex Fiction 2020
Load Bearing, first published in Ghostland Zine (issue 2) 2017
Mothering, first heard on The Paperchain Podcast 2018
Silver Birch, first published in Lucent Dreaming (issue 6) 2019
The Incorcist, first published in The Ghastling (issue 10) 2019
Wakes Week, first published in *A Box of Stars Beneath the Bed: The National Flash Fiction Day Anthology,* Gumbo Press 2016

Dedicated to the Gaslamp Writers:
Abi, Fats, Ben, Tom, Dan, Rob, Beth, & Nici,
for letting me loose and reining me in.
Thanks guys, a million times over.

Incorcisms

Acknowledgements

My thanks, primarily, to Cherry Potts for seeing the vision of this collection and making it happen.

Thanks too, to Camille Smithwick, for letting us use the image on the cover. Camille, you are the best of humans.

Big thanks to Tania Hershman. A fair few of these tales began life in her invaluable and enlightening workshops, for which I am eternally grateful.

Thanks to Dan Carpenter for commissioning *Mothering* for his *Paperchain Podcast* way back when. That was a lot of fun.

Thanks, finally, to *you* for taking a chance on this weird little collection of odd tales. Only the very finest of folks support indie presses, so pat yourself on the back and have a biscuit – you've done yourself proud.

Contents

8

The Incorcist

This is what Amy Shelling looks like now.

Pale, dishevelled, her hair pinned down but wisps of it taken up by the wind. She looks cold, doesn't she? And stressed, and tired out. She has the weight of the last nine years on her shoulders. If you look closely you can just about see the top of the scratches as they reach up her neck, but she's trying to cover them with a woollen scarf.

She hesitates on the doorstep of the terraced house. She's puzzled. Is this the place? It doesn't look right. She was expecting something more… gothic. Something grand and opulent with gargoyles and spires. It's just a terraced house.

She knocks. A woman in an apron opens the door. She has a broad smile on her face.

'Yes?'

'I'm, er… Sorry. I'm looking for… the Incorcist?'

The smile becomes a smirk of curiosity. The eyes narrow as she takes in the girl on her doorstep.

'It's Amy, isn't it? Amy Shelling?'

'Yeah.'

The woman chuckles. 'You'd better come in.'

*

This is what Amy Shelling looks like now.

She is sitting in the living room of the house and some colour has returned to her cheeks. It's warmer in here; cosy and homely. She takes her coat off, but not her scarf. She's wearing an old Adidas pullover and baggy jeans. The only skin on show is her face and hands, the two places where you won't see the scratches.

She glances around the room. Bookcase, ornaments, tasteful carpet, a clock on the mantelpiece. It is all so normal. The woman is perched on the edge of the armchair. She is fascinated by Amy. Amy doesn't quite know where to look or what to do with her hands.

'I'm so very glad you came,' says the woman.

Amy shrugs. She is blushing.

'Have you been well?'

She shrugs again and looks down at her fingers. 'It's been hard.'

'How so?'

'Everyone knows who I am. They all ask about it. Ask me how it was, what I felt like. All that stuff.'

'You're tired of it aren't you?'

'Suppose.'

'I understand.'

'Can I see him, then? The Incorcist?'

'You are quite sure, aren't you?'

'Never been more sure about anything in my life.'

The woman clasps her hands together and grins. 'Let me get you a drink. I've just made a batch of lemonade. I know it's not quite the season, but would you like some?'

Amy considers it. She's not a child any more. But she nods. 'Thanks.'

'You wait here, I'll fetch it.'

*

This is what Amy Shelling looks like now.

She's crossed to the bookshelf and we can see a bit more of her body shape now that she's up and about. Put on weight, hasn't she? She's trying to hide it under that jumper, but we can tell from the way she holds herself. It's good, it's a good thing; she looks healthier, radiant even. She's turned into quite a handsome young woman underneath all the gloom, hasn't she? A good make-over and she'll be a stunner.

'Here you are, dear,' says the woman as she comes back into the room.

Amy jumps and hurries back to her seat. The woman hands her a tall glass of lemonade. Amy takes a sip.

'Good, isn't it?'

It is good. It's very good. Amy nods and drinks some more. She feels it fizzing down her throat.

'How long has it been, Amy? Could you tell me?'

Amy licks the lemonade from her lips. 'Ten years,' she says. 'Nearly.'

The woman smiles and thinks for a moment. 'Yes,' she says. 'Nine years, nine months, nine weeks. Three nines and then… here you are.'

'Is that OK?'

'Here you are. To invert the world again.'

Amy frowns. A thought reaches her.

'It's you, isn't it? You're the Incorcist?'

The woman's smile deepens, and she nods. She still hasn't removed her apron. Amy becomes aware of the ticking of the clock on the mantelpiece.

'What compelled you, Amy? Why now?'

'I'm sick of it. All the press, the paparazzi and that.'

'Why now, specifically?'

Amy tuts and rolls her eyes. She shifts in her seat. 'I'm going on *This Morning*.'

'*This Morning*? The television programme?'

'Yeah. Schofield and Willoughby.'

'I see.' The woman sits back and considers it. The smile drops from her face, just for a few moments. It soon returns. 'Drink your lemonade, Amy.'

Amy drinks. It is delicious. She drinks again.

'Will it hurt?' she asks.

The woman reaches out and takes Amy's hand, very gently. Amy finishes her lemonade, puts the glass down, waits for something to happen.

'You have to understand,' says the woman, 'an incorcism is nothing like its counterpart. No bells and whistles, no drama. All it takes is willingness, which you already have in spades. The mere act of you coming here and knocking on my door fulfils the most dramatic requirements.'

Amy is still frowning, but something has changed.

'Can you feel it?'

The woman kisses the back of Amy's hand. It is not necessary, but she is compelled.

'It's already happened,' says Amy as she lets go. 'He's back.'

The woman takes the empty glass and moves to the door.

'Show yourself out whenever you're ready.'

*

This is what Amy Shelling looks like now.

Hold on. Wait just a moment. Wait until Phillip Schofield has finished his introduction. And… cut.

There she is. Our Amy. All grown up. She looks glamorous now, doesn't she? She's been tended to by the hair and make-up team and she actually looks her age now. A little older, in fact. She has been dressed in a summery blouse and ruby red shoes and her hair has been curled into ringlets. Her arms are bare, as she requested, and we can really see the scratch scars now, can't we? The cross-cross chaos of that ten-year-old girl from nearly ten years ago.

Phillip is ready to ask about the scars. Ready to ask her to show them. And then Holly will gently move onto deeper questions. Can you describe how it felt? Do you remember much about it? Has anything strange happened since?

But Amy is ready for everything and more. Look at her. Really look at her. This is what Amy Shelling looks like now.

Pupils just a shade blacker than they should be. The tiniest fragment of a grin at the corners of her mouth. Fingernails filed to a sharp edge.

She is wearing lip gloss which she applied herself. It is lemon flavoured.

Mayday

Today, in the village of Mayday, only ticketed tourists walk the parade route, led by dead-eyed actors in cheap costumes who spout fast and dubious facts. But the actors are bit-parts in the theatrics of Mayday herself: *England's Village of the Vanished*. The tourists frame the route on their phones. The faded bunting, the dead bulbs, the scattered pinwheels, the frayed flags. In the midst of this candy floss joy, five hundred and thirty-eight people upped and vanished, and left the streamers fluttering, the maypole creaking and the giant wicker frog, unlit, unoffered, and waiting.

Before that, in the village of Mayday, a forensic row walked the parade route, inch by painful inch. They bagged every sequin, tagged every feather, logged every stain. They cordoned the frog, probed it with cameras, noted every detail no matter how small. It had been mayday in Mayday, the festival in full burst. They filled their books, but found no bodies. And no answers. And no clues.

Before that, in the village of Mayday, a brown hare hopped the parade route. It shot from the field, in flight from a sky shadow, and cowered by the flagpole by the bridge that marked the start. Then, as the sun faded, it followed the path, nose nudging curled confetti, mouth testing fossilised apples. By the pull of some ancient mystery, it hopped the full route, the exact and correct lefts and rights; past the Flek and Shettle, past the Hangman's Nook, past Tadpole Glassware and Lily's Pad until, drawn by the waters, it leapt to the green and the grand wicker frog. It was watched the whole way by an audience of one; the sky shadow with thermalled wings and tick-tock eyes.

Before that, in the village of Mayday, six sexy teenagers stumbled upon the place in a tipsy giggle. They meandered through the parade route and at first it was all snogs and piggy-backs, sniggered shushes and macho poses. But, as they snuck deeper into the village, the exact and correct lefts and rights, they were quietened. The boys tried doors; all locked. They pushed and kicked at the Flek and Shettle to no success; even the windows refused to smash. Machismo was drained, flirtation was ceased. They felt watched. Followed. They ran to the green and screamed to a stop before the giant, fractured silhouette of the frog, the beast haloed by the moon, silver-edged, gilt, mercurial and always, always waiting. The teens fled Mayday and, over the next few days, were murdered, one-by-one, in ironic ways, by one of their mothers, or someone similar.

Before that, an old man came to Mayday clutching the name of his daughter and her likeness in charcoal. The sun was high as he reached the foot of the bridge, inches away from the start of the route. He looked at the village, frozen in time. He could see the wicker frog on the green, staring at the clouds as if praying for rain. The man knew he was on the verge of something bad. He did not enter the village that day, but promised himself he would try again. But he was an old man.

Before that, in the village of Mayday, a crowd from All Hallows marched in at twilight, farm tools raised and torches lit. Twenty men, ten women, their heads anointed, drenched, dripping with holy water. A vicar led them, cross raised, a rifle hidden in his cassock, the bullets blessed for good measure; a man only half-believed, but he was all they had. They raised hell for their neighbours and prayed to heaven for a response. But the village walls blunted their shouts, their voices skimmed off the roofs without an echo. They wanted to put their torches to the frog, but the vicar's fake seizure put the plan to a grumbled stop, and then the evening rain put out their torches. Minds fell to looting, but nothing would open, no glass would break. They skulked home, wearied. The vicar returned to his church and never again came out.

Before that, in the village of Mayday, a lone figure walked the parade route in reverse. From the frog to the bridge, the exact and correct lefts and rights, every step precisely placed. When he reached the edge of the village he looked across the fields to All Hallows, to the mountains beyond, to the sky beyond the mountains, to the dark behind the sky, and further. Then he turned on his hoof and walked the route a final time. No stragglers. Everyone accounted for. A job well done.

Before that, in the village of Mayday, the five hundred and thirty eight, the purest and angelic, the peak of perfection, pond-cleansed, nude, thrumming; each man, each woman, each child, and the ancient ratio; the span from fingertip to fingertip, from hair to toe, almost floating along the route, bodies too good for the too-solid ground. Spring air heated to summer sweats, flesh mashed flesh, hair stroked hair, fingers found holes and strings, plucked pleasures and beaten hearts, and the shrill whistle at their front which led them on, on, on, the exact and correct lefts and rights. None watched, all danced, streamers, papers, glitters flung on the beat, apples ravished by the Flek and Shettle, flies clapped between palms and licked down by sticky tongues. Blood and worse from places unseen, bones thinned and softened, muscles stretched and squeaked and twisted their dances to shapes impossible, and skin glazed then shimmered then shifted and betrayed the insides it had been charged to keep hidden. Organs glowed. Rainbowed breaths. Veins swelled with dirty waters. Frogspawn eyes. Dance on, dance on, no rest for the wickered. They fucked past the nook, gasped by the glass, were filled at Lily's then man became woman, woman became man, man and woman became both and none and, on the face of their leader, a single smile as he whistled them on and then to a stop as at last they reached the frog. Hours of silence, perfect stillness. Not a flinch, not a fidget, not a blink. Above the frog a single cloud formed from the silent rise of their fluids. It thickened, it darkened, it sagged, then it burst. The waters fell upon the frog, the wicker creaked a croak, the rain stopped. Done. Nothing to return to. Not their former selves. One by one they took to the pond. Beneath the surface, they were stripped, shrunk, amoebaed, swallowed, made gone.

Before that, in the village of Mayday, only druids walked the parade route. They let the people dance, and sing, and cheer, and drink, and kiss, and fall away into darkened corners, but they alone walked the route, the exact and correct lefts and rights. Feet bare and bleeding, backs flogged, scalps thorned. Oakflint frogs on their tongues, alive and confused. The druids hummed, resisting the urge to swallow.

Before that, in the village of Mayday, the spirits walked the parade route. A midnight procession. Felt but not seen. Moonlight channelled. Glimpsed figures. Cold silver, hot stone. Frogspawn in the ponds by morning.

Before that, a wronged angel scratched his cursed name into the pit between mountains. He dipped his severed wings into frogblood and carved flames into the meadow. The exact and correct lefts and rights. The grasses obliterated. Never recovered. A permanent signature. A place to settle. A home.

Today, in the village of Mayday, only ticketed tourists walk the parade route, led by dead-eyed actors in cheap costumes who spout fast and dubious facts.

Silver Birch

'Take a seat.'

It takes no speaking to see the doctor now. Just book online, then check-in on the touchscreen, then wait for your name, then open the door, then sit on the chair that is lower than his. She flutters down to it. He hasn't looked at her yet. He's looking at her record on the computer. Sparse, bare. She can see trees through the window. Beech and ash.

He turns to her, his smile practiced but genuine.

'What can I help you with today?'

He has a surname that she can't pronounce; another reason to be glad of the website and touchscreens. Outside, a pair of magpies shoot into the beech. She finds magpies unnerving. She sang their song once, just once, and it came true.

'Take your time.'

The smile falters a little. She focuses. She points to her mouth.

'Your tongue?' he asks.

She nods. He leans back to get an instrument, a scope of some kind with a light. His shape opens up to her; broad chest, slim waist, furred arms. His chair creaks like a straining branch. He is not handsome in this room, she thinks, but elsewhere he would be. She would like to see him poolside, or in an airport. His sweat patches are demure, in their own way.

'OK,' he says. 'Let's take a look.'

She opens her mouth. He sees it, frowns. She opens her hand too, but he doesn't look down. She pushes it out and the toothed edges tickle the joins of her lips. He is very still but his frown melts away. Outside, one magpie drops from the beech to the ground and struts.

'Can I…?'

He wants to see it medically. And she allows him that, just this once. She opens wider. He shines the torch and peers at the sutures. She has been assured they were well made. She has grown used to the weightlessness of her mouth. She understands now how central the mouth is to her whole being. How it is always there; wet, hot, hard, full, empty. A complicated landscape, like something installed as an afterthought.

'Right,' he says. He sits back. She holds up her hand. Her tongue is there. Desiccated. He doesn't take it. She lays it on his desk.

'OK,' he says. This time he means; *close your mouth*. She pulls it back in and brings her lips together. It tries to cling to her palate, but she knows how to let it fall. She waits for his questions. Eating? Drinking? Talking?

He stares at her tongue for a while then he stands, goes to the window and closes the blinds. The magpie is snapped away. He slips back into his chair, leans forward. *Here comes the lecture*, she thinks.

'Silver birch?' he asks.

Now it is her turn to stare. Eons pass in her cavemouth. He makes all manner of movements. He ruffles his hair, he laughs, he rubs his eyes, he shakes his head, he leans back, he flexes his shoulders.

'OK,' he says, with a smile.

He unlaces his shoes and, with a practiced gentleness, eases them off. He is not wearing socks. His shoes are full of soil. She smells it before she sees it and her glands squirm like earthworms. He brushes his feet clean and shows her. She smiles; her eyes fill with tears and she wishes they were sap. She wants to wake up with her eyelids stuck together, with a wren nesting in her hair, with a lover carving initials into her sturdy thigh. She opens her mouth again, pushes the leaf out.

'It's all taking too long,' he says, eventually. She agrees.

He wriggles his feet back into his shoes. She blushes while he ties his laces back up. She feels excited to see him again in the future. She wants to take him to an airport.

He gives her an ornate box and tells her to open it. His toenails, all lined up like a family in a picture book. She tips them into her hand and pockets them. She gives him the box back for her tongue. It all fits together so well.

Afterwards, she visits the beech. The magpies cackle and trill in greeting. She knows their nest is up there, but she can't see it and won't climb. There is a crack in the trunk, and she feeds it his toenails. *It's all taking too long*, she thinks but she can't stop smiling. It takes as long as it takes.

Load Bearing

She brained him with a chunk of the Berlin wall. She thought he would, at least, appreciate the symbolism.

As if to say thanks, he possessed her, just half an inch aside of her brain, where, to him, it looked like the Grotte de Lascaux, minus the horse paintings.

He helped her get rid of his body. They chose Tecate, where the Mexico wall was first breached, where another corpse wouldn't make much of a difference.

He etched himself into the walls of her brain, just his initials at first, but then hers too and a heart with an arrow through it. The image was crude but effective.

At the same time, she took to the sandstone bluffs in Frodsham, England where some of the etchings dated back to the early 1800s. Simpler folk with the same problems as her, perhaps.

She replicated his drawing on the stone without quite knowing why. She'd never felt any love for him. Her initials went above his and she dated it 1799. It was unconvincing.

They went East together, where the world still tried to exist. A man there touched her temple and said she had a djinn inside her mind. She paid him to stay quiet.

She settled by the Great Wall of China, of course, where tourism was still a thing, just about. There were plans to cut it free and take it into orbit. She didn't buy into the hype.

He left her after a few years. He rappelled down the curve of her skull and spelunked his way out of her ear. He was lucky it was night, lucky she was drunk.

He ingratiated himself into the Great Wall project and, at

the triumphant moment, sabotaged it. The wall came tumbling down like a children's game.

She missed the whole thing. Stoned out of her mind on a neural implant. When she heard, it made her laugh and she knew, just knew, he'd had a hand in it somehow.

He came back to her when she was on her death bed. It was Mars now, her home. There were walls here too because there were always walls.

He stayed outside, unsure suddenly about why he had come back. They had been the architects of each other but had never bridged the gap, never made a roof.

She knew he was there but said nothing. She had other things on her mind. She was searching, frantically, for a way out of death. For a cave to hide in.

When her body gave up, she sank down, saw glimpses of a subterranean network, but could never quite take hold, never quite knew how. If he'd have seen her, he might have helped.

He hadn't seen her. He wandered. He watched. He left their initials in sand, sometimes wrapped by hearts, sometimes not.

Mothering

After the end, there is a new start. It is not what they wanted; it is exactly what they deserved.

One of them, a human, finds the supermarket where the end started, and where the new start began. He cracks his way in, finds the preserved portmanteau of the convenience congregation lurched in perpetual conflict over cornflakes, condiments and cut-price condoms. Each figure glazed in the shrink-wrap of Armageddon, a laminated Pompeii. He is careful not to touch them, he has learned that now. The survivors learn that quickly, because survival is so fragile.

The stuff of days past lies patient on the aisles, still awaiting a sell-by date which never arrived. He adds things to his rucksack, not really sure what most of it is.

There is a voice in the air. All it says is *Don't forget Mother* then a silence, then a small squeal, then *Don't forget Mother* and repeat. He thinks it might be a clue.

He pauses in the Seasonal Aisle. He tries to feel warmth from the yellows, but the cold persists. Everything is egg-shaped. There are fragile flowers and distorted chicks and the promise of sunshine and greenery. The figures here seem more peaceful than the ones near the doors. They hold brown eggs in boxes and stare at the brands. He hopes this will be the way that he nearly dies.

But he pauses because he sees a word: Mother. He listens again to the voice: *Don't forget Mother, Don't forget Mother.* He does not know what Mother is. Perhaps that was the problem. Perhaps they all forgot Mother.

He takes hold of a bag of eggs. They are small, shiny, pink.

He tears open the bag and holds three of the eggs in his hand. He closes his fingers. He wonders if the eggs will hatch, and what will emerge if they do.

*

He wanders the aisles, fills up his rucksack and leaves it by the door. Then he goes in search of the voice. It could be important. It could be an answer.

The voice comes from speakers high up in the roof, but he knows better. He knows the voice is spoken elsewhere. He pushes through *Staff Only* doors, the portals to secrets. He finds the supermarket's shadows, he finds uniformed figures slouched on burst seats, he finds *Manager's Office*, but there's nothing useful inside except pens.

Then he finds *Control Room*. He can hear the voice behind the door. It is tiny, as if trapped. He takes out his rifle and nudges the door open. It is a room of still screens. There is a person crouched on the floor, a live one. Another survivor.

They stare at each other. The person presses buttons. One button stops the voice after *Don't forget Mother,* another creates the squeal and a third makes the voice sound again. Click, voice, click-click, voice.

'What is Mother?'

'I'm trying to remember.'

There is a crossbow on the desk. On the screens, he can see the supermarket torn apart and frozen, mis-angled and dulled.

'Should we fight?'

'No bolts.'

'No bullets.'

'No point then.'

The person stops the voice completely and rubs his face. He pushes himself from the floor and stretches his limbs.

'What's your name?' he says.

'Sophie,' he says.

'I'm Rebecca,' he says.

'Sophie, can I ask you a question?'

'Sure.'

'Have you ever had a baby?'

Sophie thinks back to when his belly burst and a baby with a string fell out, blood-red and screaming. The pain, the fear, the spillage.

'Yes,' says Sophie.

'How did it feel?'

There is something wriggling in Sophie's hand. He opens his fingers and looks down. The eggs have hatched. Three tiny baby shopping trolleys bash through the chocolate shells. Their wheels squeak and tickle Sophie's palm.

'Can I have one?' says Rebecca.

'For free?'

Rebecca nods.

'Sure,' says Sophie.

Rebecca takes the cutest one and puts it on the desk next to the crossbow. Together, they watch it skitter around. Rebecca puts it back on its wheels whenever it falls over. He seems to have forgotten about the voice.

Sophie sneaks away. He lets the other two trolleys loose into the supermarket. Whenever they touch a figure it will wake. Perhaps one of them will remember. Perhaps one of them is Mother.

But Sophie doesn't want to be here when that happens. Sophie has done his bit. He takes his rucksack and flees the place.

Daylight Savings

Sam: It's your Dad.

Jenny: Hold on a sec.

Sam: He says are you turning the clocks back?

Jenny: Just doing it!

Sam: She's just doing it, John. Yeah. Say that again?

Jenny: I'm doing it now Dad! What's the time?

Sam: He says to keep turning it. I don't know what he's on about, here.

Jenny: Hiya Dad.

John: Hello pet. Are you turning the clock back?

Jenny: Just doing it now.

John: Right well don't stop. Keep turning it.

Jenny: You what?

John: Don't stop at one hour, keep going! Turn it slowly though, take it slow.

Jenny: What you on about? Sam, what's the time?

John: Keep turning, keep going!

Sam: 10:04. No, 10:05. It's dark out. Streetlights are still on. Is that right?

Jenny: 10:05.

John: Keep turning, Jenny! Trust me pet. Keep going back. Slowly; an hour every thirty seconds.

Jenny: Dad, what are you on about? It only goes back one hour.

Sam: Is he alright?

Jenny: Dunno.

John: We're doing it, we're all doing it!

Jenny: Are you outside somewhere, Dad? You sound like you're outside. Where are you?

John: Are you still turning it?

Jenny: No.

John: Turn it, Jenny!

Jenny: Ok, alright, I'm turning it.

Sam: What's going on?

John: Take it slow. One hour every thirty seconds or so.

Jenny: He says to keep turning it.

John: Put me on speaker, love.

Jenny: Put it on speaker.

Sam: What's all this, John?

John: Hello again, Sam. Just trust me. Tell our Jenny to keep turning the clock.

Jenny: I am, Dad.

Sam: She is.

Jenny: How long for?

John: Just keep going!

Jenny: Where are you, Dad? Are you outside? You'll catch your death. Is it raining?

John: Don't worry about me, pet. Just make sure you keep turning the clock. One hour every thirty –

Jenny: Yeah, yeah, every thirty seconds, I've got it.

John: Is little Sarah there? You there Sarah?

Jenny: No, she's downstairs.

John: Fetch her up; she's got to see this. This is wonderful, magical.

Jenny: Dad, I don't understand…

John: What you on now? What time?

Jenny: Just coming up to two.

John: Great, that's great, keep that pace going.

Jenny: How long for though?

John: Is Sarah there? Fetch Sarah.

Sam: John, are you alright mate?

John: Fetch Sarah, Sam!

Sam: Alright, alright. Sarah, love! You wanna just come up here a minute, say hello to Granddad? What's this about, John?

John: Nothing short of a miracle, Sam, nothing short of a miracle. Can you see outside?

Sam: Yeah. We're in the bedroom. It's dark outside. Like middle-of-the-night dark.

John: Good, good. Just watch it though. Keep watching it.

Sarah: Hiya, Granddad.

John: Sarah, love! Hello, my sweetheart, how are you?

Sarah: I'm good thank you. Are you still sad?

Jenny: Sarah…

John: No, no thank you, Sarah, but no. I'm as happy as can be! Sarah, listen very carefully – do you have any fruit in the house? Apples or something?

Jenny: We got those bananas didn't we love?

Sarah: Bananas.

John: Perfect! You think you can run and fetch one of those bananas for me?

Sarah: For here? Like, bring it here?

John: Yes, yes! Quick as you can.

Sarah: Ok.

Jenny: Careful on the stairs Sarah, don't run. Why is it dark, Dad?

John: You'll see, you'll see. Oh! My, my, it's working, it's really…oh God!

Jenny: Dad? Dad, what is it? What's working?

John: Sorry, pet…it's just…it's really happening…

Jenny: What is? Where are you?

Sam: Come on, John, you've got to clue us in here.

John: Ok, sorry. Listen. We've been going at it, a team of us, since one in the morning. Last night. Well, tomorrow, next week, whenever it is!

Jenny: What do you mean, Dad? Have you been out all night? Up all night?

Sam: Have you been drinking, John?

John: No, no; clean as a whistle, Sam, don't you worry! I'm fine – I'm more than fine, I'm spectacular. We're all here, the whole group.

Jenny: Who are? What group?

John: Never mind about that, it's a sort of club. A society. It doesn't matter. We've been at this all night, all together – and around the world too. All synchronised.

Sarah: Banana.

John: Sarah! Great, you've got it?

Sarah: Yep. One banana.

John: Ok, put it down on the bed. What colour is it?

Sarah: Yellow.

John: Is all of it yellow?

Sarah: The top bit is a bit green.

Jenny: Sarah, is this from the fruit bowl?

Sarah: Yep.

Jenny: From the ones we bought yesterday in the shop?

Sarah: Yeah, Mummy. What?

Jenny: I bought those bananas cheap. Past their best.

John: Keep watching the banana! Are you still turning, Jenny?

Jenny: Yes, I'm turning, I'm turning.

Sam: It's getting light out.

John: Yes, Sam! And it looks like…

Sam: Evening.

John: Bingo! What colour is the banana Sarah?

Sarah: It's going green!

John: Green!

Jenny: Dad, what is this? What's going on? I don't like it!

John: Turning back time, Jenny, turning back time! We've been at it since one in the morning so we're actually a bit further back than you might think –

Sam: What the hell do you mean, John?

John: You can see it! The banana, look. It's back to – maybe four days ago? It'll get faster as you catch up with us.

Jenny: What do you mean catch up, Dad? How far back are you?

John: If the synch has gone right… we'll be coming up to twelve days back now.

Sam: Twelve days?!

Sarah: Are we time-travelling?

John: That's right, Sarah! Time-travel, like Doctor Who! Just for a bit though, not forever.

Sam: This is stupid. This is impossible. Jen, put the clock down.

John: Keep turning, Jenny.

Jenny: I am, Dad. Just tell me when.

Sam: Jen, what the fuck?

Sarah: Daddy!

Sam: Jen, put the bloody clock down.

Sarah: No, mummy, keep going!

John: That's right, pet, keep going. Keep on…oh God, that's it… keep on turning!

Sam: No. No way. This isn't right.

Jenny: Shut up, Sam. Just tell me when, Dad.

John: I will pet, I will.

Sam: No fucking way.

Jenny: Stop swearing, Sam.

Sarah: Stop swearing, Daddy!

Sam: Twelve days? Are you at the cemetery, John?

Sarah: The banana is tiny now Granddad. Just a little green stick.

Sam: Answer me, John.

John: Yes, Sam, yes. It's working.

Jenny: Is it working, Dad?

John: It's working, pet.

Sam: I can't… I can't be a part of this.

John: What's it looking like outside, Sam?

Sam: Dark, light. Dark again. Light.

John: You're catching up. It'll slow down soon. Oh my, here we go…

Sarah: Is Granddad at the cemetery Mummy?

Jenny: Yes, love. Yes, he is. Dad?

John: …

Sarah: Granddad?

John: …

Jenny: Dad, answer me. Has it worked?

John: …

Jenny: Dad?

John: I'm here, I'm here. Are you ready for this?

Sam: No way in hell, Jen, no way.

Jenny: Shut up, Sam. I'm ready, Dad. We're ready.

John: Gladys? Gladys? I've got Jen on the phone. With Sarah. They'd like to say hello.

Scaffold

After, she built a scaffold on the eastern side of her face. With the fiddly struts and the microscopic bolts, it took her most of the night and the constant deluge of rain didn't help.

The workers arrived in the morning. They blasted and scoured her, barked instructions across her pores like itches. Tarpaulin strips flapped in the gale of her breath. But the work soon paused. The foreman hauled himself to the peak of her nose. *It's the retina*, he called. *Detached. You'll need a specialist, love.*

He came the next day and invaded the jelly of her eye with as little pain as could be managed. The optic nerve was rethreaded, the retina realigned while the workers kept their chatter to a mumble, out of respect.

But the damage was too great. The specialist shuffled off, despondent, and the workers set back to the rest. The cheekbones were recoloured, the jaw bolstered, new teeth installed.

The specialist returned when the scaffold was gone. He was more casual now, as this was his day off. He was in the area, he said, and he had a thought. Well, more of a proposal; a gift, even. He would install for her, if she wanted, a blue-plaque contact lens, free of charge, if she had something she would like to memorialise?

Preserved

It was quite impossible for the same man to be in every single one of his photographs. But there he was: a thick bush of hair with a shock-white streak, a gaunt face, a lazy jaw that kept his mouth slightly open. A frown like someone interrupted, and sharp eyes which always, always found the camera.

The man had no business being there. Not only could he not have worked on so many different sites, he simply wouldn't have a place in these pits, these mines, these factories and canals. The man only had one arm. There was no employment for him.

The photographer did not panic. Instead, he cleared the floor of his studio and laid out each and every photograph he had ever taken. In each one he found the man and pressed a pin through his heart as if preserving butterflies.

He counted as he went and, when he reached his hundredth image, he started to mutter to himself: *here he is again, hello again my old friend* and; *don't you worry, he's perfectly armless.*

But, of course, he wasn't armless. He still had one arm, the left arm, and that meant he was far, far from 'armless.

There was only one thing for it. He set up the camera and pointed it at an empty chair. Compelled, he placed himself into the frame, beside the chair and asked his apprentice to take the shot.

While the picture developed, the photographer stayed very calm. Very, very calm. Blotches bloomed into shapes, the shapes shifted into a man and a chair, a man and a chair, a man and a chair. Just a chair. A normal chair with no-one on it, beneath it, or behind it. The photographer breathed out.

And then he looked at the man, at himself, at the shock-white streak in his hair, his open mouth, and the gap where his right arm should have been.

The Midnight That Never Came

The limp worsens just a fraction each day, and the seams of the briefcase strain a micromillimetre more, and it takes him just that quarter-second longer to get to spot 58, where he sits. Manuel Ortega, on his fold-up stool. He waits for a midnight that never comes. This isn't just me being all *fasiel*, I can see this detail; the worsened limp, the stitching in the seams, the timing, because that's what I'm good at. The tiny details of things, the *olio nuem* of it all. Manuel can't see it. He's too far stuck inside the bigger picture, I think. That's why we are friends now, I think.

'*Konnichiwa*, Manuel,' I say as he squeaks past and he nods at me and smiles at me, both of which are hard for him (I can see the strain in his neck and his jaw). He will leave at 12:35. Half an hour plus another five. His midnight never comes. It will never come. I'm not sure if he knows that. Those bills in the briefcase have the wrong face on them now. It is the face of a *muerten*; a man fallen to a hard death. I don't know if he knows that either.

I say to him; '*Bon nuit*, Manuel,' as he passes to go home and then I only get the nod, not the smile, and the nod is much smaller.

But tonight, there is a car. There are always cars, of course, but tonight there is one which is strange because it's been parked up in 158, right above Manuel's head, and hasn't moved for three days. I've watched it on the cameras these past nights as midnight comes, as Manuel stands up from his stool, suitcase in hand, ready. But nothing happens. I mean, of course nothing happens. But still; strange *ne*? I wait until he sits down – 12:14:33 seconds, edging ever later – then I put the 'Back in 5' sign on my booth and lope out.

'*Hola*, Manuel,' I say and this time I get a frown. He pulls the briefcase closer, just by a third of an inch. 'There is a car, upstairs.'

He doesn't understand. I mime a steering wheel and point to the ceiling. His pupils widen with thrill, with fear, with both. I put my hand up, tell him to stay where he is.

'I will go see,' I say, in my best approximation of his language. 'You wait. Yes? Wait here.'

'*Si*,' he says, and it is the first time I've ever heard him speak. His voice is so thin.

'*Si*,' I say, which means yes in neither of our languages, but it is understood. I stride the ramp to the next level up.

*

It is one of the ugly places, this multi-storey. A real *baadul-majin*. That used to be me; finger-guns firing at the places of the city. I'd wink bullets at the *majin*, click blanks of respect at the good. Then I switched sides, like we all did, and the vices versa-ed. This was a city of vice-versa until the bills changed. We're all supposed to think it's stable now. Maybe it is. Too soon to tell. *Majin*.

Look at the charging docks for electric cars. Half of them are off, many buckled from scrapes, bent like yanked statues. The floor numbers are new font, but old digits ghost through, just aside. Same with the graffiti; the sky-blue paint scheme is too thin yet to keep it all out. And there's new tags in stinking fresh, down at the south end where they've not put in the updated lights yet and all is a-flicker. That falls to me, night-watchman, but I'm not paid *fuet* to deal with that. They fly in the cans on drones and spray through templates, in and out before I can get up. What's a guy like me to do? Never fight drones, it's a *gui*'s game.

The car waits. It's from before; an oil guzzler. Five years and they'll all be gone. But there's something about this one that doesn't add up. So neatly parked. So carefully kept. Not a bump or scrape or *bauip* of rust on it anywhere. Like it's just rolled off the production line. Ah yes, and it has no plates. Taken, we think.

I circle it, three times, one for each night it's been here. Tomorrow, it'll be towed, taken to another ugly place, taken for its fate. I muttered about it to my super yesterday, said: *can I check it, cheik?* Might be new bills in it, was the implied. He shrugged his yes. So here I am, crowbar up the sleeve, a familiar strut. I let it slip down, wedge it against the boot and flick. The boot pops but doesn't rise. I'm thinking body, but that's how we all think now, nothing strange in that.

'*Jalleck,*' I say, just in case, and then, behind me:

'*Jalleck. Amnied.*'

There's Manuel, one bay back, watching.

'*Amnied,*' I say to him and he appreciates it. He is holding his briefcase, his stool. He would be incomplete without them, a half-thing; a *dersh.*

I lift the boot. No body. We breathe different breaths.

Manuel takes a few steps forward. The boot is not empty. There is a suitcase, unzipped and open, squashed clothes as stuffing. And a scattering of papers, some books, and three mobile phones, the type with buttons and tiny screens. I grab a handful of the documents. It is all in *Taink,* a formal lay-out. The letterhead is the old university, the one that held and held then fell. I dig through the clothes and find two passports, both blank. At the bottom I feel the bulge of a gun but don't reveal it. Revealed guns get fired and *majin* soon hears. I flick open the books. Various notes and receipts flutter out, in different languages. That spells a taste of sickness that I don't like. *Tow it*, I mutter to tomorrow, *tow it far*.

I see a name repeated and point at it. Manuel puts down the stool and pulls out a pair of spectacles from his top pocket. He reads the name, reads a few other words and flicks his eyebrows. He takes the spectacles off, puts them away. He tilts his head at me.

'Kkkerrkk,' he says, and whips his finger across his throat. I slam the boot shut. It is 12:36.

*

We take an easy time to stroll back down, side by side. I can hear the whistle of the breath that shoots from his nose. I offer to carry the stool, but he tuts, mutters something, laughs. He laughs like a gutter draining; from full to clean.

I wish for the Langue app, or a translator drone – or a translator person of course, of course. But there is nothing here but the two of us, the cars and the concrete. I want to say to him: *Manuel, your trips here are fasiel. We changed, ne? We tore down the man, put in another one. Both majin, both bauip, but one released us from the other. Your money will not work, your son is… I cannot say kkkerrkk.* There is too much I cannot say.

He laughs again, looks at me and I laugh back. Does he mind-read? This is the age of it, we say; all things can happen now, and will. I take the sign off and climb back into the booth. The seat shows the impression of me and I slot back in. Manuel comes to the window.

'Thank, thank,' he says, in my language. He flicks open one clip of his briefcase and fishes out two notes. He puts them on the counter. The serious face of the *muerten* stares up at me, the one whose eyes I would always cross out.

'The count will be short,' I say, in my language. He grins and taps his head then he beats a rhythm on the counter. He snatches up one of the notes and folds it carefully; two ridges which cut down along the *muerten*'s eyes and the corners of his mouth. He points at the other note and I do the same.

He leaves it at that. He touches the brim of his hat, clips the briefcase shut, toddles away. The limp is slightly better, the strain of the briefcase much, much worse.

It is 12:48. I have never needed clocks, I just know. I take up a note. I've seen this folding trick before, I remember it. I tilt the note forward and *muerten* smiles, I tilt it back and *muerten* frowns. It entertains me all shift.

In the morning, I find a quiet place, somewhere ugly, and burn them. I should not have them with me. I know how fast things can change in this city.

Turning Mermaid

She knew of a method, she said, to turn mermaid, she said;
a place in the woods, a copper bath, in the midday sun of All
Saints Day, she said, and she invoked the *I'd do anything for you,
babe* promise – something I'd said, repeatedly.

So, for once, we had a sober Halloween and we hired a van,
drove through dawn, and set up in Wych Elm Wood. This is it,
she said, heat up the water, she said, I love you, she said, while
she wriggled her toes in the carpet of leaves and muttered her
goodbyes to them.

A Remnant Low

Gaja sowed her crop of elephants through recovered fields a month before the cyclone arrived. The trunks had sprouted well, healthy and full, despite the stones. She sang her father's songs as she dripped honeydew through the nostrils and massaged the flesh with shea butter. She would smile to herself as her father's lyrics began to change. Where he crooned lost loves and bright skies, she told the trunks of the fun they were to have when they ripened and rose, of the itches they would scratch on the coconut trees. She liked her versions better.

They came to her house, urged her to leave. They showed her a future; the path of the cyclone as it would travel, slicing a neat line through the tip of her country as if to create an island. *Only three miles north*, they said, pointing west. Gaja feigned concern but it seemed like a fair distance to her. She showed them the trunks, let them help her with the honeydew and butter (although she kept the songs to herself). It did nothing to lessen their insistence. She would not be persuaded.

The storm hit on the third day of the holidays, a mile or two off from where they'd predicted. She stayed inside, as told, but could not stop herself from watching the fields. The trunks pointed west, in urgent coordination. She sang and sang, tried different songs with hasty lyrics, but the rhythms were off, the cadence wrong, and they went from her, the elephants, ripped from the ground, the weakest first, then one of the strongest, then the rest in quick chaos; the bodies pale and frail, knots of blind pink, squished up but soon so floppy as limbs peeled from bellies, and unready ears flapped open to behold the sound. Some were ripped from their trunks and tumbled alone

47

to be smashed, she imagined, on distant asphalt, against towers of cities. She watched until all were gone.

They came back three days later with supplies she didn't need. She ate with them, took their words with good grace. After, she followed them down to the beach, touched the gouges where the coconut trees had stood. They would be replanted, they assured her, plans had already been made.

Help Yourself

An ice cream van, abandoned, with a message in the windscreen. Madison and Chris found it, back from their early morning run. The cabin door was unlocked. Chris checked the ignition, found no keys. He knocked at the house opposite. Madison waited by.

Tamir answered, bleary-eyed and gowned. He knew nothing of the van. He frowned at it, as if driven straight out of his just-disturbed dream.

Chris was enthralled. He climbed in, checked the freezers. Fully stocked, he said. He told Madison she could come in. She had been waiting by. She went in.

Chris pressed at the till and the drawer pinged open. Money inside. He didn't take, but left the drawer open and kept glancing.

Madison took the message from the windscreen and unfolded it. A Samaritans leaflet.

She put it back.

She stepped out. Waited by.

Tamir stepped in, followed by his wife Garima and their two boys. Things started getting eaten. Tamir giggled as he swirled cream onto a cone, the boys grabbed two Mini-Milks each, Chris took a Calippo, Garima claimed a box of rocket lollies and a few cans of pop.

Soon, a knock on the hatch. Sonny from two doors down, Frank from thirty-six. Tamir opened the hatch, pointed at the leaflet with its magic words, laughed that laugh of his. He clapped an arm around Chris, and they started serving. No money changed hands, but a few notes slipped free of the till-drawer before Garima had sense to shut it.

Madison waited by. Said it was too early for sugar. Said to Chris she needed a shower and got his nod of approval.

She heard when Tamir got the *Greensleeves* jingle going. Heard more doors in the street opening, more voices. There was plenty to go round.

When she came back out, Cassie and Beth from thirteen were siphoning the petrol. Kids in pyjamas devoured flake-spiked monstrosities drenched in syrup and sprinkles. Fallen ices congealed in rainbow bursts.

She picked out the leaflet and held it for a while. At a quiet moment, she showed it to Chris.

Later, he seemed to blame her for souring things.

The Thrower and the Catcher

He fetches his tools from the barn and heaves the bow-ball into his truck. The light streaks stains into his hands that only rain can wash off, no tap or river. A spectral burst on his overalls, jewels clinging to his stubble. No-one sees him so no-one minds.

He sets the barometer against the sundial and measures the skies. Lines of shadow cut over numerals, the needle quivers across the bar labelled *Rain*. He uses scrappy paper and a stub of pencil to calculate the position. His finger reads this way and that across the map and he pins down on a meadow south of Pennick Tor.

He grunts. He knows it. Interesting. To the east, the mirror of Glassir Reservoir which will be calm today. To the west the ridge of Alnshot, leading to the peak of the Tor. But beyond the waters, another flat meadow. The catcher will be in clear line of sight.

He packs away the gear into the glovebox of the truck and tromps back inside. Atop the wardrobe, snug inside a brown leather pouch, an ancient pair of binoculars. He fetches them down. At his feet, his two whippets Indigo and Violet look at him with those forlorn marbles, full of questions. *Why torture yourself? What good will it do?*

He bends and fusses them, one apiece and then together. They enjoy it for a while then shrug him off and fold into baskets with huffs and snorts. It used to be he'd take them with him, the man and his hounds, their proud silhouettes. But they stay home now, it's easier that way. It's just a job that needs doing, nowt grand about it these days. No-one comes out to see his silhouette no more. Times have changed.

The binoculars clatter against his chest as he strides across the mud to his truck. The old thing takes a few turns to cough into life, but he gets it. He doesn't see the whippets watching from the window as he drives away.

*

He bumbles through the dales, across fens, stopping only for gates and to carry the bow-ball over cattle grids. He learned that one long ago when the floods near enough washed his home away. Karma's an old goat.

It is a big one today. The streak will be impressive and will stay up for long minutes. A few lucky ramblers will see the crown of it. Some of the folk down in Alnshot village might snap a picture or two. And although the work will be tough on his bones, he's glad too of the strength of it. More time for looking.

The day stays clear. He arrives, eases his truck into a shallow ditch and hefts the ball out. He carries it like a favourite dog, spits of its sparks scratching his stubble. He is aglow with its spectrum, a paused disco taken out to pasture. He sets the thing down as gently as he can manage.

Has a little look, then. A peer across the reservoir. No sign as yet, but the catcher is often a little after the thrower. He has his radio with him, charged and ready.

The stripping is violent, but no good can come of a tangled rainbow. He clamps the ball down first to hold it steady, then heaves at it with the hack-claw. Lengths strip out 'til he has something long enough to work with. Twenty metres or so. He stabs the claw into the soil and sets to attacking the knots with his thick, quick fingers. Colours unfold from colours, shades separate, the primaries hold firm and the secondaries soon follow. He mutters, tells them all about King Richard and his battle in vain.

Soon enough, it's ready. He stops for a thermos break, just a small one. Gives his toes a rub, chomps away an apple. His eyes stay fixed on the horizon and he starts to thinking; *shake it off*, but then he hears the purr of a distant engine and soon enough, his radio crackles into life.

'Come in Throwerrrr,' squalls the voice. The man is the same age as he, been doing this just as long. But he puts on like he's half the age, like this is nothing but a hobby which he can give up at any time.

'Aye,' he says in response.

'Top day for it, Tom.'

'Aye. 'Tis a nice one.' *Nice* is fine word he thinks. Better than *top*.

'Just let me get on over then I'm ready for you, old man.'

He bites the inside of his cheek and watches the approach through the binoculars. There he is, the catcher, in a beefed-up tank of a Land Rover, not a spot of dirt on it. The thing tears through the meadow like some rabid hippopotamus trying to carve out a new river. Catcher slams to a halt and leaps out. He's in new gear again; riding boots, Levi's, a leather jacket, a woollen flat cap, as inauthentic as they make 'em.

'Ready when you are, pal.'

Pal. He's got an earpiece in an' all; twisted black plastic and blue LED lights with a little stick of a microphone hovering over his cheek. He's talking as he waits, on some sort of call.

Thrower sets down the binoculars, looks at the waiting bow ball with its streak of a tail. He wants to throw the whole bastard thing over the water and smash the catcher into a billion particles of multicoloured light. But that would be too pretty an ending for him. He'd love that; out in a blaze of sparks like the last firework of Bonfire Night.

For years it's been he and him, the same trundling trucks, the same grunted *Ayes*, the ancient ways followed, the patterns undisturbed. A little pot of pounds on the porch come morning, not much, just enough to get by. And then, from nowhere, the catcher has all this shine. And other people to talk to.

'Any time you like, Thomas.'

And names. His name is not Thomas. It is so much further from Thomas than could be imagined. He tosses away the apple core and swears at the clouds. The dark ones to the east already hammering out their rains. And the sun waiting, as ever. Still a job to be done and Karma watching.

He rests the clips of the hooks into the undersides of orange and indigo and pulls the tail straight. He sets his aim right, checks his distance. Flat, clear, pure. The catcher slouches against the hood of his behemoth, doesn't even look to be facing the right direction. Thrower pumps his legs like pistons, and he hoists the tail of the rainbow high above his head. He feels the snag as the ball catches, but it all unravels true. Then he pops the triggers and the clips let go and the rainbow flies out over the waters, as free as swallows and just as swift.

The ball dances out as the ribbon-road unfurls. Between heartbeats, he grabs the end before it can flutter away. Seven quick clasps driven deep and the thing holds, proud and strong. He looks up the curve and the glow burns out the sky. It is the brightest he's seen in a long while.

'Have a good one dude,' bawls the catcher. Thrower watches the other tear away, a new trench carved, a kicked gust of white smoke shot back to smear at the bow. Something inside the thrower cracks. He grabs up his rucksack, packs it tight and runs back to his truck. A few frantic tugs of the ignition and the old thing grumbles into life. He floors the pedal, bounces from the ditch, and follows.

*

Catcher drives fast, of course, but thrower keeps up. The monster vehicle is hard to miss. They've never met in person before, know nothing much of each other's lives beyond what they've gleaned down the years, and what they know of the job. The thrower gets the delivery and takes it to the spot. The catcher gets the signal and must be in the right place, right time. They each collect their clamps back after the rains and the sun have passed.

No need for the telling of the job to no-one else. Both get paid the same, the thrower a little more, but not by much. Simple lives. Keep selves to selves. Take a partner, someone meek, someone mild. The thrower had never found such a person, but had his dogs.

Catcher leads him through the next village to the new development one stop over. Thrower slows as catcher pulls off road to a gravelly driveway, to a large iron gate, to a mansion beyond. There is no other word for it. Mansion. All long windows, columns, marble statues, shaped bushes. There is a child out front playing with a drone.

Thrower parks across the road and strides over, but the gate is closed when he gets there. There's a buzzer to one side which he presses, but when the thing sounds all his nerve is shot out. A woman answers.

'Hello?'

He says nothing.

'Can I help you, love? I can see you. On the camera.'

He ducks his head, shuffles. His overalls are streaked in fading strips of basic colour.

'You a friend of Tony's?'

Thrower scuttles away. He darts back to his truck, dives in, swears an almighty litany at the ignition then gets as far away as fast as he can, the wrong direction for miles and miles.

*

An hour later, he heads back to the meadow to fetch his clamps. He is so fixated on the road, on the depths of it and the things it could tell him if only he could hear, that he does not see the flailing rainbow straight away. He's back in the ditch before he sees whipping violet, and the red smashing at the clouds. At first he wants to scream the murder of the catcher to the gods, but it is not the catcher's side which is loose, it is his own.

He runs to his clamps and tries to catch the flailing tendrils, but they thrash too high for him to reach. There is nothing to do but release the other clamps and speed around the reservoir to collect the ball from the other side. He flicks them off without thinking for too long. The green strip lashes him, coats him in its lightning slime, knocks him clean off his feet. The final clamp, indigo, gives way under the pressure of the whipping and the metal thing is flung from the ground and nearly takes off his head.

He hammers the truck into life and speeds out to the catcher's meadow. The bow has arced over and lies writhing among the mud and the struggling grass. There is no time to see if anyone has noticed, no time to put anything right.

He uses his hack-claw to drag the bow back into a ball and heaves the frazzling thing into his truck. He speeds away, ears twitching for the sound of the catcher coming back for his clamps, but the other man doesn't show.

*

He puts the bow in his front garden, hoping and praying that it will fade. He scribbles a note of apology and traps it under a milk bottle on his porch. He will expect no gold in the morning, that much he's clear on.

No sleep comes for him that night. The dogs whine their worries with each toss and turn. Waking dreams see the catcher bashing at his door, fistfuls of multicoloured grass stained for eternity, and a raging sun raining hot lava upon his forehead. He sees Karma too, an old goat, nudging a nose against a fallen rainbow, anger flaring in its eyes.

In the morning, the bow-ball is still there but it is monochrome; five greys, a black, a white. There is no pot of pounds. The note has gone; taken perhaps, or escaped with the wind and flung away.

'No' Has Too Much of a Habit of Knowing in Advance

Throw chains around the house; the kind magicians use for water tanks. But these must be real, no tricks; links the size of elephant heads, links for hoisting anchors on prison ships; pull them tight against the bricks, crush the gutters, snap the tiling, squeeze the breath out of the place. A *no* has been sounded, an unequivocal no, the kind that needs the locks we ask for. We've moved the Dickensons out of 13 and Shirley in 17 says she doesn't mind a bit of disruption as long as it doesn't cost her anything and none of the rubble falls in her begonias (which it won't, if you follow our designs precisely). Think of what you might need for such a job and then treble it; the cost is not an issue. Doors and windows should be unbudgeable and we will not tolerate gaps for squeezing through, or under, or over. When the locks have fastened, melt down the keys.

We're sharing watch duties while we wait. It was a *no* that scoured the street, you understand; we were like dogs and distant fireworks, the nervy kind, the yappers. We muttered a strained *fifteen* in monotone because we know what has become of that place, the one cloaked in the shade of some tree planted eons ago. There is no tree. We had the tree removed. It made no difference.

NO, came the sound in all-caps; the dead-call, the kind that has a habit of knowing in advance. The kind where the *N* thinks it is a genesis, a seed of all being, and the *O* is the void upon which it reigns down its hammer blow. Fused, they make a thing which is both unmoveable object and unstoppable force; an ungodly collaboration which rends the earth in two. That should give you a better sense of the kind of chains we mean. Cataclysm withstanders. Three sets.

You might hope, of course, to stage a rescue first. We strongly advise against it. One more of those *NO*s and the whole street will collapse. It's understandable and, believe us, we've had the same thought many a time. But ours is not to interfere, merely to contain. The damage has long been done. And yes, we understand that this advice itself is like a version of the *NO*, and it might make us look a bit mob-like, a bit pitchforks and torches. But our *no* is different. Look at it. Gentler, softer, a little vulnerable perhaps. We're asking you to please consider our feelings. We simply cannot stand the situation any longer and something needs to be done. The chains should do it. They are the best our murmurs and flicked eyebrows could come up with at such short notice. We'll pay premium for fast delivery.

Wakes Week

Sis can't talk much because of her phossy jaw. She got her phossy jaw from the matches she makes in her factory. It made a hole in her face and I don't like looking at it. She don't like talking now, because of her phossy jaw.

It's Wakes Week in Bury. We have the week off to do other things. I don't know what to do. Sis tries to sell matches in the streets, so I help her. She don't sell many. I ask her why it's called Wakes Week. She holds a hand to her jaw and says; *it's when the world wakes up.*

I don't understand. She says she'll show me. She stands one end of the street and I stay at the other. She waves and I can still see her, and I wave too. The air has gone away. I can see all the way along the streets now.

Then she takes me to the roof of the factory. It's dangerous and not allowed, but I trust Sis and she smiles to show me it's ok. I can see a long, long way. It is the most beautiful thing I've ever seen, apart from when Sis didn't have her phossy jaw.

We count the chimneys. There are lots and lots, more than ten. I only thought there was two: mine and Sis's. But there are lots and lots, more than ten. She sits me on her knee and holds up my hand and we point at the chimneys and she tells me where they are. *That one's Preston, that one's Blackpool, that one's Burnley, that one's Accrington, that one's Bolton, that one's Wigan, that one's Stalybridge.*

I know it hurts Sis to say these words, but it is brilliant to see the whole world wake up. It is all factories like ours, and I think that is amazing. I wonder if there is anyone in the world who could fix Sis's phossy jaw, so I ask her, but she shakes her

61

head and frowns. I know what that means. It means: *stop asking questions now.*

So, I stop asking questions. Instead, I count the chimneys again. There are lots and lots, more than ten.

Different, Somehow

When the Turnbulls got back from the holiday, things were different, somehow.

Cameron heard it in the bedroom. He hauled the suitcase onto the bed and… he wasn't sure. Something in the bounce of the mattress? Or… it was the soft squeak of the springs. They sounded… what? Off-key? He pushed the suitcase down, let it go, listened. It was like someone had been sleeping here. Or… shagging here? No. More like someone jumping up and down on it and –

'You alright, hun?'

Layla tasted it in the water. She'd been desperate to get back to her own taps after the harder stuff in the Cornwall B&B. She'd gone straight to the kitchen and gulped down two glasses and… what? It tasted… off? Could water be off? She drank a little more. Metallic? It was almost as if she had a tiny cut on her tongue, or had burned the roof of her mouth, but she'd done neither of those things. And was it even the right colour? It looked –

'Muuuum? Hellooooo?'

Katya felt it in the bathroom. She went to the shower as soon as she could to wash off the six sticky hours trapped in the car with only her brother's stench for company. But she couldn't quite get the temperature right, and when the glass of the cubicle misted up there was… what? A message? She ducked and leaned and squinted but she couldn't tell if the gaps were letters or… symbols? Weird little pictures? The water stung her skin, way too hot – or was that just the sunburn on her back? And then she was struggling to breathe. The steam was catching in her throat. Can steam even do that or –

'Neeed the toilet, Katyaa!'

Bobby sensed it in the garden. Weeds he'd never seen before, bees avoiding certain flowers, grass blades all at different lengths, and the single dried-out worm on the middle stepping-stone, right where he'd left it a week ago. He checked for the blackbird in the hedge. The nest was still there but no bird. He scraped up the worm, took the crab shell from his pocket, and put them both in the nest with a few whispered Bobbywords. Something had gone sideways. He needed to be ready.

'Oy.' It was Koli, peering over the fence.

'What's going on?' said Bobby.

Koli smirked. 'Police. Looking for a body. You missed all the fun, Bobster. Come on, I'll show ya.'

He went to fetch Shuri from her basket, but she wasn't there. He found her cowering in the airing cupboard.

'It's sideways,' he said, in their language. 'Koli knows a deadness. We'll balance things.'

Shuri wasn't convinced but she was glad to leave the house. The air in there was… whiny, tail-droop, hackled.

Different, somehow.